P9-BYB-475

PRINCE BERTRAM THE BAD

by
ARNOLD LOBEL

HARPER & ROW, PUBLISHERS
NEW YORK AND EVANSTON

To my grandparents

PRINCE BERTRAM THE BAD
 For information address Harper & Row, Publishers, Inc., 10 East 53rd Street, New York, N.Y. 10022.

Standard Book Number 06-023975-1 (Trade Edition)
Standard Book Number 06-023976-X (Harpercrest Edition)

LIBRARY OF CONGRESS CATALOG CARD NUMBER: 63-8471

PRINCE BERTRAM THE BAD

Once upon a time a prince was born. "Long live Prince Bertram!" shouted all the people in the kingdom. His mother and father, the king and queen, were very happy and proud.

But Prince Bertram was not a good baby. In his crib in the royal nursery he cried all the time.

When his mother took him to the park, Prince Bertram was not friendly to the other babies.

Even before he was old enough to walk, he had torn up all of the roses in the royal garden.

The king and queen hoped that Prince Bertram would grow up to be a good boy. But as each year passed, he grew meaner and naughtier. He had a whole roomful of toys and he had broken every one.

The royal coachman did not like Prince Bertram. He would ride through the town blowing pebbles at the people with his peashooter.

The royal cook would not speak to
Prince Bertram. He had thrown
four spiders into the chicken noodle soup.

The swans in the royal lake would not swim near Prince Bertram.
He made terrible noises and horrible faces to frighten them.

"If only a spanking would do some good." The king sighed. His hands were red and sore because he had to spank Prince Bertram every day.

Of all the children in the whole kingdom there was not one who was as mean and as nasty as Prince Bertram. Everyone called him Prince Bertram the Bad.

One morning
Prince Bertram
sat in the
highest castle
tower hitting
the birds with
stones from his
slingshot.

He saw a large, long-nosed
black bird in the sky and
hit it, too.

It was not a long-nosed black bird at all but a witch,
who was passing by on her broomstick.

The witch was very angry with Prince Bertram. She pointed a finger at him and shouted, "ALAGABIM."
Prince Bertram was quickly changed into a small scaly dragon. "That will teach you to throw stones at me," said the witch as she flew away.

"Mama, Papa . . . Help!" called Prince Bertram.
The king and queen were startled.
"What has happened to our boy?" they cried.
Clouds of smoke and fire came out of Prince Bertram's mouth.
"What shall we do?" shouted the queen. "He will set fire
to all the window curtains!"

"That boy has been acting like a beast for so long that he has turned into a dragon," said all of the people in the kingdom. "There's nothing left of Prince Bertram but the crown on his head." Everyone thought it was a great joke, and they came to the castle every day to laugh at him. Prince Bertram was tired of being laughed at. He was a very unhappy dragon.

One night he took some gingersnaps
from the royal pantry and ran away.
There was a big forest near the castle,
where many lions and porcupines and other beasts
lived. The animals growled and roared at him,
and they ate all of his gingersnaps.

The animals thought he was strange and no one would play with him. Even the birds made fun of him. Prince Bertram was lonely and sad.

Soon winter came. The wind grew cold, and the snow began to fall. Prince Bertram tried to keep himself warm with the fire from his breath. He wished that he were safely home in the castle with his mother and father.

On the coldest day of the winter Prince Bertram was walking through the forest, looking for something to eat. Suddenly he saw two legs with shoes on them sticking out of a snowbank.

Prince Bertram dug into the snow and was surprised to find the very same witch who had changed him into a dragon. She had lost her way while flying through a snowstorm and had fallen, broomstick and all, into a deep snowbank. Prince Bertram quickly opened his mouth and blew a big breath of hot fire and smoke at her. The fire melted the ice and the witch opened her eyes.

"You saved my life," said the witch.
"Dear dragon, what is your name?"
"I used to be Prince Bertram until I threw a stone at you,"
said Prince Bertram sadly.
The witch remembered what she had done.
"Bless my broom," she said, "even witches make mistakes."
She pointed a finger and shouted, "ALAGABOOP!"
At once Prince Bertram was a boy again.

The witch flew Prince Bertram home,
and the king and queen were
overjoyed to see him.

The witch stayed for lunch.

Then she gave Prince Bertram and his mother and father
a ride on her broom.
As they flew over the kingdom the people cried,
"Look, Prince Bertram has come back, and he is no longer a beast."

That night at bedtime Prince Bertram
heard a voice outside his window.
"Good-bye, Bert, and stay well," said the witch.
Then she flew off into the evening sky.